MR.WRONG

by Roger Hargreaves

WORLD INTERNATIONAL

Whatever Mr Wrong did was absolutely, totally, completely, utterly wrong.

However hard he tried, he just couldn't do anything right.

Just look at his house!

One fine morning Mr Wrong woke up.

He hadn't slept very well because of the way he'd made his bed the day before.

He jumped out of bed, fell over (twice), put on his shoes (on the wrong feet), went to the bathroom (tripping over the bathmat), squeezed out some toothpaste (on to the wrong side of his toothbrush), cleaned his teeth (ouch) and went downstairs.

Bump, bump, bump, bump, bump, bump, bump!

Not a very good start to the day.

In fact, his usual wrong start to the day.

In his kitchen, Mr Wrong poured some milk on to his cornflakes.

And missed!

As he sat in his kitchen, that fine morning, eating his dry cornflakes, he sighed.

"Oh dear," he thought, "I do so wish that everything I do wasn't quite so absolutely, totally, completely, utterly wrong."

So, after breakfast, he went for a walk in order to think how he could solve his problem.

It took him ten minutes to get out of the house, because he kept trying to open his front door outwards instead of inwards!

As he walked along he passed a worm.

"Good morning, Dog," he said.

The worm grinned.

He was used to Mr Wrong.

He met a postman.

"Good morning, Mr Wrong," called the postman cheerfully.

"Good morning, Doctor," replied Mr Wrong.

Oh dear!

He met old Mrs Twinkle who lived down the lane.

"Good morning, Mr Wrong," she smiled.

"Good morning, Mr Twinkle," replied Mr Wrong.

Oh dear!

And then he met somebody he'd never met before.

Somebody who sort of looked like him, but didn't.

"Good morning, Sir," said that somebody.

"Good morning, Madam," replied Mr Wrong. "I'm Mr Wrong."

"I guessed that," replied the person. "Well, I'm Mr Right."

"Now tell me," he went on, "why are you walking along looking so miserable?"

"Because," replied Mr Wrong, "I can't do anything right!"

"In which case," said Mr Right, "we'd better do something about it. Follow me."

And off he set.

And off set Mr Wrong.

In the opposite direction!

Mr Right hurried back, and turned him round.

"This way," he said, and they walked together to where Mr Right lived.

It was a house which somehow looked something like Mr Wrong's house.

But different.

Mr Right took Mr Wrong into his living room.

"I think," he said, "that the only way you are ever going to change is for you to come and live with me for a while, and you may end up being not quite so absolutely, totally, completely, utterly wrong about everything."

"Sit down," he said, "and we'll talk about it."

Mr Wrong sat down.

And missed!

Mr Wrong stayed with Mr Right for a month.

And, during that time, he changed.

After one week he was slightly less wrong than he had been before.

After two weeks he was even more slightly less wrong than he had been before.

And, after a whole four weeks, he was a changed Mr Man.

You could hardly tell the difference between him and Mr Right.

Don't you agree?

Mr Right was delighted.

"Told you," he cried. "Told you that everything about you might end up being not quite so absolutely, totally, completely, utterly wrong!"

"In fact," he continued, "you've really turned out all right!"

Mr Wrong blushed.

It was quite the nicest thing anyone had ever said to him in the whole of his life.

And he went home.

And lived happily, and right, ever after.

Now.

You probably think that's the end of the story.

Don't you?

Well it isn't!

And the reason it isn't is because of what happened to Mr Right.

The trouble was, you see, that the longer Mr Wrong had stayed with Mr Right, and the more right Mr Wrong became, the more wrong Mr Right had become.

Isn't that extraordinary?

"Oh dear," Mr Right sighed. "My plan didn't quite work out the way I'd planned it after all."

And he went to bed.

In the bath!

3 Great Offers For Mr Men Fans

1 Token
EGMONT WORLD

1 FREE Door Hangers and Posters

In every Mr Men and Little Miss Book like this one you will find a special token. Collect 6 and we will send you either a brilliant Mr Men or Little Miss poster and a Mr Men or Little Miss double sided, full colour, bedroom door hanger. Apply using the coupon overleaf, enclosing six tokens and a 50p coin for your choice of two items.

Egmont World tokens can be used towards any other Egmont World / World International token scheme promotions., in early learning and story / activity books.

Posters: Tick your preferred choice of either Mr Men ☐ or Little Miss ☐

Door Hangers: Choose from: Mr. Nosey & Mr Muddle ☐, Mr Greedy & Mr Lazy ☐, Mr Tickle & Mr Grumpy ☐, Mr Slow & Mr Busy ☐, Mr Messy & Mr Quiet ☐, Mr Perfect & Mr Forgetful ☐, Little Miss Fun & Little Miss Late ☐, Little Miss Helpful & Little Miss Tidy ☐, Little Miss Busy & Little Miss Brainy ☐, Little Miss Star & Little Miss Fun ☐.
(Please tick)

2 Mr Men Library Boxes

Keep your growing collection of Mr Men and Little Miss books in these superb library boxes. With an integral carrying handle and stay-closed fastener, these full colour, plastic boxes are fantastic. They are just £5.49 each including postage. Order overleaf.

3 Join The Club

To join the fantastic Mr Men & Little Miss Club, check out the page overleaf NOW!

Join Our Club!

MR.MEN & Little Miss CLUB

When you become a member of the fantastic Mr Men and Little Miss Club you'll receive a personal letter from Mr Happy and Little Miss Giggles, a club badge with your name, and a superb Welcome Pack (pictured below right).

You'll also get birthday and Christmas cards from the Mr Men and Little Misses, 2 newsletters crammed with special offers, privileges and news, and a copy of the 12 page Mr Men catalogue which includes great party ideas.

If it were on sale in the shops, the Welcome Pack alone might cost around £13. But a year's membership is just £9.99 (plus 73p postage) with a 14 day money-back guarantee if you are not delighted!

HOW TO APPLY To apply for any of these three great offers, ask an adult to complete the coupon below and send it with appropriate payment and tokens (where required) to: **Mr Men Offers, PO Box 7, Manchester M19 2HD.** Credit card orders for Club membership ONLY by telephone, please call: **01403 242727.**

To be completed by an adult

❏ **1.** Please send a poster and door hanger as selected overleaf. I enclose six tokens and a 50p coin for post (coin not required if you are also taking up 2. or 3. below).

❏ **2.** Please send ___ Mr Men Library case(s) and ___ Little Miss Library case(s) at £5.49 each.

❏ **3.** Please enrol the following in the Mr Men & Little Miss Club at £10.72 (inc postage)

Fan's Name:_____Fan's Address:_____

_____

_____Post Code:_____Date of birth:___/___/___

Your Name:_____Your Address:_____

Post Code:_____Name of parent or guardian (if not you):_____

Total amount due: £_____ (£5.49 per Library Case, £10.72 per Club membership)

❏ I enclose a cheque or postal order payable to Egmont World Limited.

❏ Please charge my MasterCard / Visa account.

Card number: | | | | | | | | | | | | | | | | |

Expiry Date: ___/___   Signature: _____

Data Protection Act: If you do **not** wish to receive other family offers from us or companies we recommend, please tick this box ❏. Offer applies to UK only